The Missing Reel and Unknown Witnesses

Two Horror Stories

Fredrick Niles, Christopher Besonen

Fever Garden Publishing

The Missing Reel and Unknown Witnesses: Two Horror Stories

ISBN: 978-1-950021-18-5

FEVER GARDEN PUBLISHING

First edition. March 28, 2025.

Introduction

If I'm being honest, I had a hard time remembering whether it was Chris or me who had the idea to do a collaborative effort. So I dug back—*way* back—through some messages and found that it was something that came together rather naturally back in 2022. Chris mentioned he was thinking of working on a few collaborative efforts and then I told him that I always had about a hundred book ideas floating around in my head and that I'd probably hit him up at some point about working on one.

Ironically, every project we've worked on to date has been one of his ideas. I think this works out well because Chris, at heart, is a short fiction writer. His prose style and imagination are closer to that of John of Patmos than Stephen King and most of his published works are either short stories or novellas. I, on the other hand, have the toxic trait of imagining every possible story idea as a six-book series of full-length novels.

In a yet-to-be-published work between the two of us, Chris had this great idea of someone who fishes confessions out of murderers and serial killers via a magic pool full of dead bodies. He sent me roughly 8,000 words, consisting of a neat beginning, middle, and end. That was about three years ago at this point and last I checked, the project is currently sitting at 72,000 words and still needs some expansion in the epilogue.

We've had a few other ideas that we worked on together for a bit but quietly shelved them in favor of *actually* releasing a short story first instead of trying to blow everything up into something ten times larger than the original work. So that was how *The Missing Reel* came to be.

The Missing Reel was originally an idea that Chris had about a YouTuber walking through a haunted asylum that was actually haunted. He banged out a solid 4,000 words and then I added another 4,000 worth of backstory, dialogue, and internal monologue. All in all, I think it turned out pretty well and I gave myself a nice little pat on the back for being restrained enough to simply double it in length instead of whisking it off into the woods for five years only to return with an unrecognizable behemoth that swallows raccoons whole and can't fit inside of a standard 4-door sedan.

We released the story to Godless.com as an exclusive digital short and received quite a positive response from the indie horror community. Now was the perfect time to release the other story Chris had sent me that I had ballooned up into a full-length novel. Unfortunately, it takes a long time to proof and edit a novel and we opted to push that to the back burner .

Instead, Chris pitched another idea, this one focusing on a group of people who don't know they just witnessed an abduction. I told him that it sounded awesome and could very easily be written as a full-length thriller novel, to which he replied something along the lines of "Please stop." So we agreed to keep it short story length. He worked on it a little bit, sending me snippets throughout the following weeks. And then I had the idea to turn it into something like a found transcript.

Chris agreed. We went over who was going to cover which perspectives, separating them equally between the two of us, and then we got to work. The story came together quickly and naturally. We passed it back and forth a few times. And then we finally scheduled a date to meet (digitally) and edit the thing.

Our editing process is somewhat maddening, consisting of screenshots passed back and forth between the two of us via Messenger. Chris questions my word choice about a hundred times (rightfully so, more often than not) and I bring a big black metaphorical gun to murder all of his commas (no regrets). We quibble over a few things, make some compromises, and then BANG. We're done.

(Next time we're just doing a shared Google Doc.)

We released *Unknown Witnesses* as a Godless.com digital exclusive on the exact same day as we had *The Missing Reel* one year prior. We didn't do it on purpose but the sequence of events played out almost identically. Chris said we should have it ready for Halloween. I dragged my feet until the last minute. We asked Drew Stepek over at Godless if they had any openings for new releases at the end of October. They're a horror platform so *obviously* they did not. Then we followed up asking when the next available date was and it just so happened to be November 2nd both times.

Nice. Like it was meant to be.

Looking at the page count of each story now, we realized that we had enough to go ahead and put together a physical copy. We tried to do it earlier with *The Missing Reel* but came up just barely short, which was another motivating factor for writing another short story.

It occurred to Chris that these two stories have no narrative thread connecting the two and that folks might question why they are combined into a single book as they are, to which I said, "I'll just write an introduction. I reckon it'll be fine then."

So there you have it: the story of how *The Missing Reel, Unknown Witnesses*, and this introduction all came into being. We hope you enjoy these tales and we look forward to continuing on into a long and fruitful future of collaborative releases. (At least, whenever we get around to editing that novel.)

-Fredrick Niles

The Missing Reel

"Welcome. I'm excited to host your channel here to-day. Pity that your wife could not make it."

"Yeah, well, she had a prior engagement. It is what it is."

"I'm sure we'll have you back. Assuming you'll want to come back."

"I love all things spooky. I'm really looking forward to shooting this video and showing the viewers the art of your scares."

"Let's waste no time then. Is the camera rolling?"

"It is. I can edit the excess. I'm ready to explore your haunt. I've heard nothing but fantastic reviews. I also heard it takes a while to get through and even with a full battery no one's been able to film to the end. Trying to avoid that mishap during my visit."

"The place is rather large, but that's not what drains the battery. No, the culprits for such shenanigans are our extras."

"Extras?"

"Additional scare actors, if you will. There are no employees here today, but you may come across once-living frights. Just be alert. When you review your footage, watch closely and you may see things that you missed."

"Good sell, man. I'm spooked. Look, I now have goose-bumps. You're suggesting to me that your haunt is literally haunted?"

"You can tell me after you've finished the experience. This is, 'Earth's Fingers,' a tyrant in the name of terror. After their visit, eleven people committed suicide, each leaving notes behind that put the blame directly on my attraction."

"Really? I didn't come across that info during my research."

"I had it buried, sealed. Bad press is not something that I can tolerate. I couldn't risk being closed. You'll need to edit this bit out, obviously. I have to stay open, not only for me and the artwork inside but for all of the cast that reside here without pay."

"You mean the ghosts, right?"

"You give me your honest review after your experience here has settled in. I don't want to give you expectations of what may or may not occur today."

"Fair. Let me do my intro, then we can start..."

***

"Thanks for coming on yet another journey. Today, we find ourselves about to embark on a lights-on tour of Earth's Fingers, a botanical horror experience. I am here with the brain behind this operation and we are going to see what a legendary attraction like this looks like without the fog, strange lighting, and scare actors. Instead, we are getting a behind-the-scenes look at this 'by invitation only' attraction and guess what, you're coming with us!"

Jesse steadied his camera, then paused for a moment so that later he could edit in his channel's introduction, then he panned the lens to show the vine-ridden front of the asylum that had grown over so much that the haunt didn't even have a sign visible. The outside looked like a run-down mental ward but as soon as the door opened, the horror enthusiast gasped.

"I'll leave you to it," the owner said, dismissing himself. "But don't be surprised if I pop up from time to time. For your purposes, a few things might need context."

After he had left, Jesse began his trek through the asylum.

"Whoa, I'm losing my gourd already," he chuckled to the audience, a large grin on his face as he weaved in and out of a hallway of black-eyed children.

Some of the children were short, some were naturally tall, some were on varying heights of stilts, but each of them had their hands reaching outwards with their chests opening up like blooming flowers. Some of their limbs extended in awkward ways like uncontrolled branches. Though none of them moved in full motion, Jesse could almost feel their stares as if they were living. They watched him as he passed, their eyeballs so lifelike that he anticipated one of them blinking abruptly.

The flesh of the children in the hall was ingrained with strands of moss, the veins of their bare feet rooted in the ground.

Different species of flowers grew out from under the skin, making them look as one with the haunt.

Some of their mouths had spirals of vines crawling from them that connected to the various plant life that was plastered all over the walls and ceiling. Strobes flashed when motion was detected. This was likely meant to disorient the passing thrill seekers, but being a lights-on tour, they had little effect.

"This is freaking amazing," he said to the camera, his lens taking in the breathtaking scenes.

The hall of kids opened up to a room with walls that expanded upwards and then narrowed, making Jesse feel like he was being enveloped by them. There were a few spots where he could tell an actor would be placed but they were currently empty. The floor beneath him creaked.

Jesse looked down and saw that the floorboards were completely buried in trampled flowers. Adding in to the creep factor were the rocking chairs. In some sat animatronics, while others were barren and likely meant for actors to sit in. One of them even fell apart and then completely reassembled itself.

Wires, Jesse thought to himself. *Or maybe magnets.*

Whatever it was, it made for an elaborate display. A small and intricate touch to an already impressive presentation.

The chairs were all made up of tree bark and looked hand-carved, but many spots resembled plant varieties. He couldn't name any of them but he bet that his wife, Mikaela, could have if she had been here.

Leaves crunched beneath his feet as he walked. They were brown, orange, and red. Fall tinted. He imagined Mikaela kicking her way through them the way she did every Autumn when they would fall off the big maple in their backyard.

It made him miss her.

He would bring her back here, he decided. She would love it. She had wanted to come this time but the invitation was last minute and she had prior engagements to uphold. A work friend's wedding. Jesse was thankful to be here and not trying to make small talk with couples he barely knew.

"Details are astounding," he said off-camera, showing the scenery before him to his future viewers.

The room got smaller as Jesse went on and just as he was about to enter a corridor, he saw a streak of green strands out of the corner of his eye. The movement was rapid and he felt bummed that the camera was fixated in the opposite direction. He jerked the camera to where he had seen the movement but everything was still.

After a few seconds passed, he moved on with his tour. He looked over his shoulder a few times to see if he could catch sight of whatever he had seen before but the hall behind him was empty. Turning back, he saw more movement on the walls and flinched. Something deep inside of him roiled with disgust.

Termites. The room was full of them. How the place kept from collapsing around him, he didn't know. Maybe the vines held it all together, which wasn't a reassuring thought.

The next area appeared to have a miniature big top circus tent jammed into the room and upon entry, Jesse immediately recoiled. In addition to what looked like a ragged and decomposing assortment of circus paraphernalia, there was a vast network of poisonous herbs interwoven with the display.

The pathways were clearly marked out by a thin rope about three feet high that gave a decent amount of room for the visitors to walk without coming in contact with the plants. Even so, Jesse's mind wandered back to the waiver he had had to sign when accepting the tour.

As horrible as the place looked, it was also strangely beautiful. Strange and alien flora seemed to sprout from every possible crevice. Blooming in the center of the flowers were clown faces. Some smiled while others frowned. He wasn't sure what they were made of or how Richard, the owner, had accomplished such a thing but it must have been an enormously tedious task.

Jesse looked up and saw that children covered in rashes from the overgrown ivy plants had been sewn into the big top. Some of the bodies hung from the ceiling with botanical nooses around their necks and he had to maneuver himself and the camera around their dangling feet.

The big top led to a long hall of more kids with terrible rashes covering their anatomies. Some of them were shrieking silently from the irritation. Jesse could see sores in their mouths and throats. They looked real, every detail intricately placed to show their shrieks of despair. Some of them held plant-covered boxes that were probably supposed to pop out freaky clowns, but the lids were too tightly enclosed by herbal matter to open so the contents remained hidden.

For the first time since entering the haunt, Jesse found himself wondering about the validity of the place's "ghosts." He considered himself a pretty open-minded guy and certainly wasn't against the idea of some sort of spiritual plane that the dead inhabited, but he had never come up against the idea in such a way.

Most of the stuff had to be fake, he figured. But then again, a haunted house attraction was just the sort of place that might obfuscate an actual paranormal reality. And if there was ever a place to be haunted by ghosts, Jesse figured it was this one.

The invitation he had received came in the form of an email. Jesse and Mikaela got invitations to places all the time that were supposed to be haunted, but they had to pass on a good deal of them. Lots from folks who didn't feel comfortable sleeping in a house that someone had died in and tried to make something of it. Even more places that were just opening up and looking for a quick hit of publicity. Even after many reminders to their audience that they were not a paranormal channel, the invitations still stacked up.

Most of the inquiries were duds. Cheap attractions or old houses that looked creepy on the outside but were pretty mundane and harmless inside. When Jesse had done a search on this place though, it struck him that Earth's Fingers was the real deal. If not actually haunted, the place was at least something of an online phenomenon.

Most of the reviews for the place were raving, with a minority that seemed to have been written by people who were genuinely upset. In the haunted house realm, it was always difficult to tell if that was a good thing or a bad thing. As Jesse continued to dig into the building's history however, he found himself getting more and more drawn in.

The original structure had been erected in 1918 as a children's asylum. Not much news on the place until 1972 when a series of deaths occurred and the place had to be shut down. Apparently, 34 patients and 11 staff members were killed due to "contaminated drinking water." There were also reports of a gas leak and a fire. A few articles attributed all this to a major shift in the building's foundation. There were a few investigations that didn't lead anywhere but the prevailing theory was that an underground river had eroded away the bedrock and loosened a footing beneath the building.

The place was shut down and the EPA investigated the property and surrounding areas for water contamination and turned up nothing.

Jesse had then moved onto some discussion forums about the incident and was bombarded by a tidal wave of insane conspiracy theories ranging from the asylum being a test center for the CIA to it being the battleground of an interdimensional war.

Jesse quickly moved on to a few articles from 1987, where it was bought by a retired botanist who was looking to turn the building into a florist shop. In an interview, she spoke about how the town had seen a massive increase in botanical activity over the last couple decades, pointing out that a strawberry the size of a human fist had just won a blue ribbon at the county fair the previous Fall. A strawberry that had been picked in a ditch right across the road from the asylum.

The botanist had tested the soil in the area and confirmed that there was indeed a high degree of fertility in the land surrounding the place. She opened the business in the Spring of 1987 and by the Summer of 1988, she and two others were dead. A murder-suicide, the papers called it, though there was some conjecture around one of the bodies that appeared to have been hung from the rafters by a thick vine.

The story tickled the back of Jesse's mind as he considered the bodies hanging from the top of the circus tent. With a place such as this, it was difficult to draw the line between a tasteless joke and a macabre acknowledgment of the place's history.

Eventually the owner, Richard Parks, had come along and transformed the place into the sensation that Jesse saw now. The haunt hadn't garnered any national acclaim yet but if Richard could manage to go the next few years without getting sued, then there would certainly be a fair level of recognition.

Jesse wondered about the guests who had killed themselves. What could have been so troubling that they would take their own lives? Richard had said that those records had been sealed but Jesse had his doubts. It was difficult to erase every trace of something like that in today's digital age and he made a note to dig into it a bit more when he got back home.

He didn't want to cause any trouble for the man but if something nefarious had taken place, then there could be a bigger story underneath all of this than just a tour of a haunted house.

"Truly terrifying," he chuckled at the audience, his camera lens investigating the decorations with precision.

As the lens passed one of the kids in the wall, Jesse could have sworn he saw the child wink. He spun his camera around but it was too late. The child was still. If it moved as he saw it, the camera didn't catch it. He hoped that the footage replay would at least show that the kid was now facing the other way.

Zooming in, he realized that the boy's hands were made of branches. Gnarly and untrimmed, they seemed old but alive. They were neatly folded over each other but he imagined them reaching out to grasp at him. To hold him tight. To squeeze his throat.

He didn't know where the image came from and he immediately forced it down. He couldn't be losing it this early into the walkthrough. He needed to slow down and catch his breath, maybe have a drink of water.

He had no water though and the clock was ticking, every passing second further depleting his camera's battery. He'd have to keep an eye on it. Maybe swap it out somewhere down the path. For now though, he would focus on continuing through the forestry ahead.

The flowers went from poisonous to large, their epicenters all smiling jesters. In their leafy hands were surgical instruments that gleamed with the fractured light of the aged lightbulbs hanging above. The lights looked vintage, and if they were, Jesse pondered on what they had seen in years past.

The deeper he went into the haunt, the more overgrown it became. He had almost missed the multi-colored lightbulbs that were hidden in the greenery. Every tile and crevice was filled with some kind of plant and they all smelled very real to him. A delicate mixture of sweetness and rose scent, with an underlying current of damp dirt and decay. He felt pollen tickle his nose and fought to keep from sneezing.

As his eyes watered, he saw a blurry face. A big smile, framed by dangling green hair. He wiped at his eyes furiously and blinked away the tears. The face was gone.

"Mikaela!" He yelled, but no response came. His head felt like it was swimming so he slowed down a bit. The walls around him seemed to pulse, then feelings of love and fear for Mikaela suddenly surged up inside of him.

Was he losing it or was she *actually* here? It was possible that she had snuck in to mess with him somehow but he sincerely hoped not and doubted the plausibility. It would make for a good video if she was playing some sort of prank on him, however humiliating it might be, but between the lucid visions and poisonous plants, there was an element of real danger for her in this place. If she really was here then he hoped she had at least conferred with the owner and wasn't just stumbling blindly through this botanical maze.

Jesse scoffed at himself silently and shook his head. Mikaela wasn't here. His sight was playing tricks on him and that was it. It was this place. The dark corners and optical illusions. He was simply bringing his own fears and anxieties in here and projecting them out onto this strange, strange world that Richard had curated.

Continuing down the hallway, Jesse found himself in a spinning room with enlarged Venus flytraps that seemed to respond to him as he walked by. He wasn't sure if it was because they were alive or if they were simply motion-activated, but the effect was incredibly unnerving. He made sure to get a long, sweeping shot of all of them as he walked on.

The next area was full of skeletons made from flower petals. They were being entangled by large trees that were growing diagonally out of the corners of the room. The angles of the trees made them look like crooked fingers and Jesse felt something click into place in his mind.

"And here are the titular *Earth's Fingers*," he said for his future audience as he zoomed out to capture the full scope of the room. The sight was truly breathtaking. Up until now, he had yet to see growth of this magnitude. There were a lot of plants and vines and giant flowers before, yes, but this was on an entirely different scale.

Jesse turned slowly, contemplating the area. He wasn't sure but it felt as if he had reached the center of the building. He considered the different sections of the asylum for a moment. The dead leaves. The carnival. All of those images had evoked something in him. Memories of sitting in the bleachers in high school, Mikaela wrapped tightly to him beneath a blanket. The last bonfires of the year. California had a notoriously warm Fall, but the rituals were the same all over the country.

When Jesse had accepted the invitation to Earth's Fingers, he hadn't expected his visit to affect him so personally. Waves of nostalgia washed over him as he remembered the first buds of romance he had felt so many years ago. Seeing Mikaela's face. Falling for her smile. Nothing like the smile he had seen here. The Mikaela that seemed to inhabit Earth's fingers was somehow more nefarious. Like some siren leading him deeper into the belly of the beast.

So far, the journey into the heart of the building had been full of twists and turns. Hallways winding around corners. Spinning rooms. It was all very disorienting. All in all, an extremely roundabout path, especially considering the traditionally block-like utilitarian nature of an asylum. The plants seemed to have transformed the place somehow, confusing the geography. What once were probably uniform rooms, all differed in size now. You either got a case of kenophobia or claustrophobia. There was no in-between.

The building no longer felt like a building. It didn't even feel like a jungle or forest. It felt closer to something like a human mind. A tangled pathway of botanical neurons and synapses. To put it bluntly, the place felt *alive*. It felt *conscious*. And the grasping wooden fingers in the middle gave Jesse the feeling that the consciousness was in some sort of starving agony. Like it was clawing to get out.

Jesse turned back around towards the Spring room, his camera turning with him. Then, for just a moment, he saw Mikaela's face pop out from behind a plant. She winked at him, then went back behind the vast wall of leaves.

His camera had caught the whole thing, he was sure of it this time. He kept his focus on filming, but in the back of his mind he couldn't wait to go back over the footage and see what it showed. Did he just catch definitive proof of a paranormal occurrence, or was it just his mind playing tricks on him? Hell, it still could have been Mikaela playing a trick on him, but he didn't think so. Her mannerisms had been odd. She hadn't moved like a normal human might move, certainly not in the ways *his* Mikaela moved. He wasn't running a paranormal channel but anything dark and eerie was fitting for his own lost soul and that of his audience alike.

"This place is tripping me out, my gourd is lost," he admitted to the camera.

Jesse turned back and continued on passed the grasping trees and went into the next room.

"Bizarre! Oh, wow!" he exclaimed as he entered. He panned the camera across a room full of mannequins that were peeling off their own skin. But their skin wasn't skin. It was moss that resembled dark, green spider webs. The scene sat against a backdrop of beautiful floral arrangements, mostly orange and brown in hue. They looked attached to what was once a cafeteria. Where overhead pipes were once connected, there now hung natural bouquets.

"Okay, I've never seen anything quite like this place. The hands, whoa, I mean, just look at the attention given to making them realistic. Very effective, especially when you add in actual actors. Really makes them blend," Jesse admired out loud as he zoomed in to examine the mannequins' hands closely and clearly.

The colors were gorgeous but the scene was seriously weird. There was no denying the aroma of this area. Whatever might have been fake in this place, the flowers definitely weren't. Jesse made a mental note to ask the owner about what was real and what was prop.

As he narrated his walk through the room, the flowers seemed to respond to his voice. They opened and bloomed, looking almost engorged. Faint colors drifted up from the petals and he felt his head begin to swim again, so he picked up the pace.

The floral path was short, thankfully, and he soon found himself walking in a pumpkin patch that was wildly overgrown. Several realistic-looking mannequins were being torn in half by the overgrown patch. The "gore" in the room was excessive. Entrails and vines were wildly entangled all across the floor and one had to be careful of their footing in here. Jesse filmed by instinct, keeping his focus on where he was placing his feet. Then, he heard a giggle that made him stop and glance hastily around.

"Mikaela?"

No response, but he both jumped and screamed an expletive when the owner came up behind him and placed a hand on his shoulder.

"Sorry to startle you," Richard stated with a grin hidden in the corners of his mouth.

"It's okay, I think my mind is playing tricks. I ventured here alone but I swear that my wife is being channeled into this place, crazy as it sounds."

"Not unheard of here. Visitors often mention seeing apparitions and mirages of those closest to them. Perhaps, the ghosts here are fans of your program."

Jesse smiled big, his dimples showing as he shook his head in agreement. What a cool idea to have reached not only the living but also the dead.

"That's bad booty, sir," he proudly exclaimed. "Bad freakin' booty!"

The owner grinned wider.

"So, in case you didn't notice—but given your obsession with Halloween I would assume that you did—you have just passed through the Autumn section," the temporary tour guide explained as they exited the grisly pumpkin patch area.

Jesse cackled, throwing his hand up to animate his mind exploding.

"The colors and themes had me feeling familiar and nostalgic earlier, but I thought that it was just me. I didn't realize that it was intentional. That's really neat. You're telling me everything is laid out according to the seasons?"

"Yes. This is a year-round haunt. We want to welcome the discomfort of horror and the ravenous ability of nature to flourish, all the time. Happy Halloween, Jesse."

"This place, it is one of the neatest spots that this channel has visited. Mikaela must come with me next time. I love it, and I wanted to ask, which of the plants and flowers are real?"

"Everything that you see is our Earth doing what it would if our species suddenly ceased to exist."

"I'm not sure I understand what you mean by that."

Richard just smiled.

"The corpses, so very life-like," Jesse admired, turning to assess them. "Also real?"

But when he turned back, Jesse found the owner gone. *Must have ducked into a boo-hole somewhere.*

"It will be if *you* die here," the voice of his wife echoed through the room, her lime green strands of hair moving along the thicket that took up the preceding room.

Jesse blinked, trying to ignore the voice this time. Trying to disregard what was surely a trick of his imagination. Then, something pushed him from behind and he half-fell, half-leapt forward.

Stumbling into the next room, Jesse felt something that felt very much like those same strands of hair tickle the back of his neck, causing him to get intense chills. He yelped, then tried to turn the sound into a chuckle.

"I don't know what's happening here but-"

Hands burst out of a messy collection of branches to grasp at him. He couldn't tell if they were robotic, or paranormal, or what. All he knew, was that they looked incredibly lifelike. He jumped aside, barely avoiding the grasping fingers.

"What the-" He kicked at the hands and they instantly withdrew back into the thicket. Kicking some more, he discovered there was nothing but brick behind the branches.

Trying to push his heart rate down to an acceptable level, he took a few seconds to observe the dense underbrush.

Chopped body parts were ingrained in the tangled up trees, some of the hearts beating as if they were still alive. As he was panning the camera, something tapped his left shoulder. Turning slowly, he came face-to-face with Mikaela, only she was made up of bark and dripping what looked like some sort of pus.

She blew him a kiss, then his camera died. The image of her was no more, but the hearts continued to thump rapidly.

"What the heckins..." he gasped, an expression of fascination and astonishment stretched across his features.

He had brought a spare battery, two of them, in preparation for such a phenomenon. He wiped his brow, took a deep breath, switched out the power sources, and then headed into Spring.

Floral owls sat on thick branches, the nocturnal anatomies consisting of marijuana buds. The smell was dank and skunky. Dewy, almost.

There was a heavy mist all throughout the room and just barely visible inside of it was Mikaela. She led the camera forward, her beckoning hand motions limbless so that only her lime-colored fingers and face were displayed. What should have been her body was nothing more than the green vines of her hair that floated along an invisible current.

Other ghastly faces were among hers. They snarled silently and clacked their jaws at Jesse as he was drawn through the otherworldly mist. He wasn't sure if the air lingered with fog or smoke, but the narrow hall went on unchanging for a few minutes before opening up to a meadow of spirits that brought a refreshing scent to his nose. Their limbs constricted, they were held to the ground by dry moss. Their expressions were of sorrow, their ascension denied by Mother Nature who held them in her floral purgatory. Wailing was heard from every direction, the camera's small digital display trembling from the vocal progressions. Everything was too real.

"Haunting," was all Jesse managed to utter.

He no longer felt like he was on a tour. He felt like he was in a dream. Bits and pieces of previous realities floated around him like the detritus of a shattered world washed up on some distant Eldritch shoreline.

He walked along the blooming, wet petals trying to decide if the scene was beautiful or unsettling. The flowery blends of the meadow really made the room stand out to the eye but the facial features of those caught in the elongated stems were heart-shattering. Their eyes fixated somewhere above, begging for assistance. Their bodies were ensnared by a naturally occurring prison. The tips of their fingers were stretched to the ceiling but they were overtaken and ascending no farther. The meadow was far and wide, the spirits equal in number to the blades of grass in the scene. Jesse filmed each one, taking his time to hone in on the realness of the facial features.

"The detail here...I've seen a ton of amazing artwork on my adventures to different attractions over the years, some exceptionally done, but Earth's Fingers has to be the most attuned to detail that I've personally come across. The camera probably doesn't do it justice but just look at the lines and grooves of decorative woe. It is something that makes this haunt special. A little more spooky."

He looked up from the camera and thought for a moment. Thought about voicing his fear that everything he was seeing was in his head and that the camera was actually picking up nothing. But if that *wasn't* the case. If he actually *was* seeing all of this, then what to make of Mikaela?

The way she had presented herself most recently was beyond some sort of prank. What he had seen as she reached towards him with hands made of bark...

It was too real. Too tactile.

So what then? Did he hope all of his experiences here were real or hallucinatory? He couldn't say. All there was, he supposed, was to make it to the end and observe the footage later.

Spring ended abruptly at the far edge of the meadow, as did the saturated breeze. In their place, was a freezing wind that sent shivers through Jesse's body and set his lips trembling.

"One thing I'll say, this haunt really touches all the senses and emotions," he admitted to his audience.

Ice glistened off the trees. The ceiling was all icicle stems, dangling from them were blue and white bats whose wings were not leathery but delicate like petals. Some of the night fliers spread their wings and ice-cold pollen rained down upon Jesse and his camera. He could see his breath; it froze upon exhaling, then broke upon his face as he continued forward. In the exhaled breaths, he again saw Mikaela and the sinister growlers, but now they were laughing at him.

"I really hope that the camera is picking up on the extra activity beyond the Winter scenery here. I love the snow dinosaurs and monsters that are devouring the kids at the playground, but I'm not alone and haven't been throughout this place, so I am hopeful that it is translating to you, the viewer, as you watch this walkthrough. I'm also seeing what appear to be ghosts peek at me from behind the carved equipment. They hide when I see them. Pretty sure that I got footage of at least three of them. If you see them when this is uploaded, please leave a comment to let me know."

There were snowmen on the backs of the creatures attacking the play area. It appeared as if they were plucking the eyeballs from the children and stringing them up overhead like reels of Christmas lights. What was more startling was the fact that the eyeballs actually emitted light. They were flashing mechanically, lighting the sky with dashes of greens and reds.

Suddenly, Jesse felt countless sets of invisible hands at his throat. They pressed, squeezed, groped, and strangled him. The camera fell to the ground as he fought to pry the unseen fingers away but he was outnumbered. He thrashed and struggled but more and more hands seemed to find him until he was rooted to the spot. Unable to move, air whistled through his constricted windpipe.

He stopped moving and the invisible hands ceased their squeezing. Frozen in place, his lungs wheezing, he glanced around.

In the distance was a toy store for customers to peruse through but the door was shut. In the backdrop of the fake business were beautiful mountains and glaciers adorned with perennial beasts that shimmered under the pulsing eyes in the ceiling. When the store door opened, out strolled the owner. In his hands was a rag doll that looked like Mikaela, the lime green hair was unmistakable on the ragged cotton head.

"Are you enjoying my haunt?"

Jesse felt the hands ease their grip on him, his breathing returning to normal. Still, his heart hammered in his chest.

"It is extremely difficult to put how I'm feeling into words," he choked, trying not to feel upset.

He suddenly realized he was free to move. Also, he felt as if the hands had never been on him, calling his own senses into question. His own memory and perception. He reached up and rubbed his throat.

"Very good artwork and scenes of carnage," he said slowly, not quite comfortable enough to relay what he had just experienced. Or thought he had. "Some of the best I've seen. I'll say it now, this place is without a doubt *haunted*."

"Seen things that you can't explain, have you?"

"Saw, felt, heard. What's the backstory?"

"Keep going, through the toy store, over the ice rink, past the impaling tree, and on into Summer."

Jesse didn't want to do any of that. In fact, all he wanted to do was leave. He wanted to get in his car and call Mikaela. He'd call again and again, leaving dozens of voicemails if he had to. He just wanted to hear her voice. Wanted to know that she was alright.

But he wouldn't. He couldn't. The channel was everything. This *video* was everything, provided the footage came out well enough. Even in the midst of all of his fear and apprehension, there was still that small voice at the back of his head telling him how good of an opportunity this was. How fantastic this experience would end up being if it would only translate to film. Mikaela herself would marvel at the footage if the paranormal things came across properly to the viewer.

"A bit of mystery, okay, I'm with it." He reached down and picked up the camera he had dropped earlier. "Let's venture into the... oh come on, for the love of Pete."

Jesse had another drained battery. He wondered if it was the cold conditions or the faces now forming on the frosty windows of the storefront. The fading expressions warned him to turn back and he wasn't sure if they were a part of the act or not.

He looked up and saw that the owner had disappeared again, leaving behind the strange doll of his wife. He bent down and picked it up, turning it over in his hand. He honestly had no idea what to make of it.

After taking a moment to swap batteries, he looked at the toy shop that had been impossibly erected inside of the building. The cramped storefront was nothing but vines and critters, all living. As he stepped inside, he realized that the vines were making their way in as well. They snaked through the cracks in the brickwork, taking control of the toys and turning them murderous.

He saw that a train track was looped around the animatronic playthings. A burning Santa was being slain in a sleigh by a jack-in-the-box toy and a black flower was growing out of his burnt rubber skull. There were empty boxes on springs throughout the aisles where actors could hide.

Jesse held the Mikaela doll in one hand, his camera in the other. He panned over killer toys that were assaulting shoppers. Pools of presumably fake blood spread across the floor and shelves. The lights flickered, an effect that couldn't be controlled due to the dictating plant life. In the flashes, he again saw Mikaela, this time she was in a block of ice and pleading to her husband to thaw her out. Her frostbitten lips mouthed for him to help her.

He ignored it.

He hated to see the love of his life displayed grotesquely, even if it was paranormal pranking. And that is what it had to be, he had decided. The whole place was too much to be a farce. Too real. Too personal. But who had ever heard of ghosts being used as an attraction? If the hallucinations were real, then what were these disembodied spirits getting out of this?

Jesse's mind flashed back once again to the people who had killed themselves. To the place's ugly history. For a moment, he felt a real, nearly paralyzing hesitancy.

He pictured the vines. The reaching fingers in the center of the building. The way the place had wormed its way inside of his head. How he seemed to be going forward in spite of everything, almost involuntarily.

Then something seemed to fog over inside of him, replacing fear with a sort of numbness. The numbness transformed into nagging curiosity, his reticence jammed down into a dark closet at the back of his mind.

There was a momentary feeling of someone inside of his head. Moving things around. Pulling levers. Organizing it like a cluttered room. Shifting thoughts and desires. And his next desire was to continue onward. To forget the feeling. To ignore the dread that echoed far off in his mind like a dog shut up in a back room, persistent but dulled.

Jesse smiled and continued on.

He focused on the people being mauled by children's novelties. He marveled at the killings, they were all so very lifelike.

Those carrying out the kills were clearly toys but their victims were almost flesh.

The back of the store was made to look demolished. The monstrous branches from a massive pine were bursting through, opening the haunt up to an ice rink of wet-clothed skaters. Most were trying to get away from the tree as it impaled them. Those not stabbed through had their hands stuck to the ice, their arms ripped from their sockets and their torsos wrapped up in coiled branches. Pine cones littered the rink, as did gallons of spilled blood.

All of the victims seemed to be wearing a sort of uniform. Something between plain clothes and hospital garb. Starchy whites like the fleece of tiny lambs, spattered with each others' blood.

Those who did not fall victim to the tree were hit by icicles flying off the rapidly spinning merry-go-round in the center. There were no survivors. Several random shrubs that strongly resembled fingers had grabbed those trying to escape the vicious pine tree. It looked like a Christmas massacre.

Jesse took the path into the trunk of the tree and it led him away from the cold to a hallway of melting mirrors. Dozens of dried-up Mikaelas were warped in the drooping reflections, her cracked lips making kissing faces at him as the cuts seeped blood. Jesse began to sweat as he kept on, ignoring the mummified look of his wife. The frames of the mirrors were cacti, which Jesse found to be very sharp after bumping into one.

He stopped to assess the tiny wound. Not much blood, all-in-all, but he noticed a few drops had fallen down onto the Mikaela-doll's face. He tried to smudge the drops away but only managed to smear them, making crimson streaks on her cotton skin.

He continued on.

The walls were all mirrors within mirrors, creating optical Illusions and giving the extras plenty to work with. The hall opened up to a barren space with scorching heat, the clutter of dead plants scattered about. Thick, wet air radiated from the room along with the scent of decay.

"Really messing with the sense of smell in here," he said to the camera. "The rot is dense."

Jesse covered his nose, trying not to gag on screen then stepped into the room.

The stench was overwhelming and he retched silently into his palm. He appeared to be in a cemetery with a climate that had the look of a desert, but the feel of a jungle. The air was thick and humid. Moist sand lined the floor, as did many filled burial plots.

In the invitation email, the owner had mentioned the tombstones. He had said that, like many of the paranormal attractions there, they weren't of his own construction and that he had found them upon purchasing the property. What was strange though, was that all of the dates on the stones were later than the purchase date.

After reading the invitation, Jesse had written the comment off as just some bit of fabricated "lore" to help sell the video. But now, he wasn't so sure. The tombstones looked real. He had seen a lot of haunt props over the years and knew how hard it was to achieve that sort of aged effect on real stone.

Before confirming the inscriptions however, he panned the camera around the room, taking in the scenery.

The ceiling was lined with heat lamps which fed the heat-tolerant plants that grew all around the memorial sites. Outstretched petals and stems reached upward, giving Jesse the impression that they were praising the light. Maybe they were. Maybe it was a sort of thank you for allowing them to take root in all who had died in the asylum over the years.

Then, he saw something that abruptly made him stop. A sight his brain had initially disregarded as just more wild plant life. But this wasn't just plant life. It was Mikaela.

She sat there on the ground, unmoving and covered in vines. Her eyes were large and staring up at him, all traces of mischief wiped away now. Her stomach appeared to have been opened, botanical intestines spilling out over the dirt and hanging down into an open grave, one of two that she was sitting next to.

The phrases, "Here lies Jesse" and "Here lies Mikaela" were etched into their respective tombstones.

"*What do I do*?" Mikaela croaked, holding handfuls of her own leafy intestines. "*I don't know what to do.*"

"What happened?" It was all Jesse could manage.

"The boy," she said, tears welling. "The one who was instituted. The one they experimented on."

"What boy? What are you talking about?"

"The one with branches for fingers. He... he killed them all. And he's here. He's still *here*."

"Where? Jesse turned to look around.

"*Everywhere.*"

Jesse turned back to look down just as Mikaela's body crumbled into rotten leaves and bone mulch. He reached out to grab for her, but all he managed to grasp was decomposing plant matter.

Something caught in his throat as he twisted to stare down into the open graves. The ones with future death dates carved into them. With *their names* carved into them.

"Room for two," the owner snickered from behind Jesse, starting up a chainsaw.

The sight was so shocking that Jesse actually felt something break inside of him. Some semblance of believability. The shattering of a mirage.

He almost laughed. After all of this meticulous construction. After making him literally question his own sanity. The owner ended the tour by starting up a chainsaw? It was the oldest trick in the book when it came to haunted houses.

Jesse aimed the lens at the psychopath and felt the chuckle die in his throat as the camera focused. Normally, the chainsaws in haunted houses had their chains removed, making them nothing more than a piece of vibrating metal. But as he focused in on the edge of the saw, Jesse saw the teeth were still there, whipping round and round in a deadly blur. The saw roared as Richard slashed it downward, just barely avoiding the removal of Jesse's hands from his wrists. He stumbled backward as his camera slid apart and fell to the ground.

Then, as if snapping out of some sort of daze, Jesse's legs took over. Forgetting the camera. Forgetting the video and the severed reel. Forgetting everything but the basic will to survive, he turned on his heels and bolted for the nearest exit.

Nothing stopped him. No plants wrapped around him. No grasping fingers.

He glanced back at his fallen camera only once. With his evidence split by the whirring teeth, he had nothing for proof. He had followed the owner from a faraway meeting spot, no address had been given that he might have been able to give the authorities. He'd be lucky if he could find his way *out*, much less back.

Fresh air and daylight washed over him as he staggered out into the parking lot. The saw roared behind him, prompting his run to turn into an all-out sprint.

His hands fumbled at the door handle, and he quickly realized it was locked.

The sound of the chainsaw ripped through the air. Closer this time.

Without thinking, Jesse dropped the Mikaela doll into the dirt of the parking lot and used both free hands to fish around in his pockets until he finally produced his car keys. He hit the fob, the locks making a *chunk-chunk* sound as they disengaged. The greatest sound he had ever heard.

Before he could even fully collapse into the driver seat or close the door, the key was turning in the ignition. He threw the gearshift into drive and the sound of the chainsaw drowned out the rattling spray of gravel as the car's wheels spun in place. A shadow darkened the driver's seat an instant before the tires caught and sent the car rocketing off down the road.

Jesse drove for a few miles at about sixty miles an hour, which was quite an accomplishment for the windy backroads. As the space between him and the asylum grew, however, the overwhelming dread he had felt slowly died down to an icy sweat.

He focused on his breathing. Steady. In and out. Ease off the pedal. Slow and gentle. *Good*.

It occurred to Jesse that he had fled so hastily that he hadn't stopped to consider where he was or where he was going. *Oh well*, he thought. He'd hit a connecting highway eventually. He had to. But the fact that he had no idea where he was also confirmed his fear that he wouldn't be able to find his way back to the place with the authorities.

There were the news articles online depicting the place's location but the town had shifted and changed a lot since then. There seemed to be little to no development around the old asylum and he wasn't sure how likely he was to find someone who knew of the place's exact coordinates.

Oh Hell, he thought. *Surely there is someone in town who remembers buying plants at the greenhouse a few decades ago.*

They have to remember. No one forgets the location of a haunted greenhouse they visited just before the owner kills two people and then herself. That's the sort of thing people cling to forever.

Even as he fantasized about finding the place again, twenty cop cars in tow, Jesse felt something poking him in the thigh.

At first, he thought it was the Mikaela doll he had picked up. But no, he had dropped that. A hot, irrational fear swept over him upon that realization. He couldn't say why but leaving the doll there felt as if he was abandoning Mikaela in some way. As if she was now left to the whims of a madman with an army of ghosts at his disposal. As if there was now a thread stretching between Jesse and Richard. A thread that he couldn't cut or run away from.

And that thread—somehow, in some way—was Mikaela.

With trembling hands, Jesse reached in his pocket and pulled out a business card. On it was a single short sentence.

"See you soon."

The words were written in a neat calligraphy, with clipped stems and flower petals drawn into the looping letters.

Jesse pressed down on the gas pedal. He felt like throwing up. Felt like choking. Like those invisible hands were on him again.

His car shot down the forest road, the branches of the trees around him seeming to wave as he passed.

Unknown Witnesses

On the morning of January 4th, 2024; Manhattan resident, Amy Fisher, and three unnamed accomplices broke into an unmarked server farm in upstate New York where they proceeded to hack and download a multitude of sealed police documents ranging from the year 1875 all the way up to the present day.

Fisher was later apprehended at her place of residence but not before uploading a number of the documents to various websites and forums across the dark web. Many of the files were corrupted while other documents were fragmented to begin with. But with the tireless help of countless anonymous individuals around the world, several accounts were pieced together chronologically from what was left.

What you are about to read concerns the events of Sonja Bixby's disappearance in the spring of 2023. Various police transcripts have been compiled for this purpose and while the information relayed here is far from the whole truth, it is enough to provide a glimpse into the strange events surrounding the case that have been erased from both independent and mainstream media sites and suppressed on all major social media platforms.

Note that while some of the formatting changes throughout, this is not due to tampering or duplication but rather the stylistic choices of the individuals transcribing them.

Amy Fisher has not been heard from since the time of her arrest. All of her socials have been scrubbed and every trace of her job history, driving record, and medical data have been erased. If anyone has any information as to her whereabouts, please email Aw8ingkingarthur@Scepter88.com

Blessings,

SwordMouth

Interview with Hannah Drake

Q=Det. Curtis Nolan

A=Hannah Drake

***=Pause

Q: Today is April 14th, 2023, and the time is 4:37 pm. We are in interview room number three at the headquarters of the Glenview Police Department. I am Detective Curtis Nolan, badge number 16743. I am interviewing Hannah Drake, date of birth 11-13-1993. Hannah, are you aware that this interview is being recorded?

A: Yes.

Q: And do you acknowledge that you were previously advised of your constitutional rights, that you signed a statement that detailed those rights, and that you agreed to speak to us without an attorney present?

A: Yes.

Q: Okay. So, you were at the Whiteset Creek playground with your son?

A: Jason, yeah.

Q: Jason. Okay.

A: His father's out of town. It's always hard to occupy kids in the middle of the day without just plopping them down in front of the TV or something.

Q: Not a fan of TV parenting?

A: No, not if I can help it. I think it messes with their development, you know?

Q: So you take him to the park a lot?

A: As much as I can. I imagine things will change next year once he starts kindergarten full-time. He's just part-time at Smithnora right now.

Q: That's the private school?

A: Yeah. Expensive, but worth it.

Q: Would you say you recognize most of the families that come to the playground?

A: Most of them. I recognized Sonja and her mom.

Q: They were there often?

A: We'd see them there every couple of weeks.

Q: As often as other families?

A: No, I kind of got the feeling that they would only go there when Sonja was driving her mom crazy.

Q: Why do you say that?

A: Well, you know, she always had this sort of glazed look about her. Like she was burnt out and just needed to get out of the house.

Q: Jennifer Bixby, you mean.

A: Is that Sonja's mom's name?

Q: Yes. You didn't know that?

A: We never really spoke. She barely paid attention to poor Sonja. There were a few times I had to resolve some conflicts for Sonja.

Q: Conflicts?

A: Yeah, like one time a kid pushed her off the ladder leading up to the slide and she started crying. I looked over to see if her mom was going to check on her but she had her head back on the bench with her eyes closed. Totally asleep. So, I ran over and made sure Sonja was okay. Then I reamed out the little devil who pushed her.

Q: Do you remember the kid's name?

A: That pushed her?

Q: Yes.

A: No, not really. Hadn't seen him before and haven't seen him since.

Q: You said "conflicts." Were there more?

A: Yeah, none that I can really think of at the moment.

Q: Can you try?

A: You know, just kids stuff. She got in a fight with a little girl over a toy a few years ago.

Q: How did that go?

A: About as you'd expect. I wasn't sure whose toy it actually was so I just walked over and calmly asked if they could share. They both pouted and eventually, the other girl walked away with the toy. Sonja didn't protest at all so I figured she was the instigator. Other kid probably dropped the toy and Sonja found it and started playing with it. Didn't want to give it up when the girl came back.

Q: Did you see Sonja instigate a lot of things?

A: No, not really. She kept very much to herself. Pretty shy girl. Didn't usually make a lot of noise unless she was crying. Then she'd ball her eyes out.

Q: And do you remember the other girl's name?

A: The one with the toy?

Q: Yes.

A: Why? Do you think Sonja was abducted by a seven-year-old?

Q: Just gathering information.

A: Her name is Trixie Martell. A very nice girl from a nice family. Nothing to worry about.

Q: You know the Martell family?

A: We've talked at the park.

Q: What do you think of them? Other than "nice," I mean.

A: Pretty well put-together. They both work hard. She's a waitress, I think. And he does carpentry.

Q: Christina and Angelo?

A: Yeah, have you talked with them? Chris was there this morning.

Q: We haven't concluded our initial interviews yet.

A: Ah, well she'd be good to talk to. I think Angelo was there too, actually. They both watch Trixie like a hawk.

Q: They might notice someone who looks off?

A: Definitely.

Q: How about yourself? Did you notice anyone who seemed off?

A: Not that I can think of. I was just watching Jason and then Sonja's mom started yelling. Asking if anyone had seen her daughter.

Q: Do you know what time this was about?

A: 11:30ish. I know because we were about to head back to get started making lunch.

Q: And you didn't see anything?

A: Nope.

Q: Sonja just disappeared in broad daylight with a bunch of families there?

***

Q: It's okay, take your time. Just think. What did you see?

A: I saw Jason over on the slide. I think Sonja was on the swing set last time I saw her.

Q: The swing set. That's next to the parking lot?

A: Yeah. Oh! There was a van!

Q: A van.

A: Yeah, but not like a white panel van that you see in the movies. It was a brown thing. Kind of beat up.

Q: Make and model?

A: Chrysler? Not sure. I remember it because it had been there when we got there earlier. It was just us and another family. The other family had walked so I remember wondering who it belonged to. It was kind of like--well, there was something about it.

Q: Like what?

A: You'll think I'm stupid.

Q: I won't.

A: Well, you know how sometimes you can look at a car and even though you don't see anyone in it, it feels like it's not empty?

Q: Sure.

A: Well, that's what this felt like. Like there was someone in it. I didn't look in the windows or anything but I think someone could have been in back. There weren't any windows back there and it looked like the sort of thing someone who's hard-up might live out of.

{Remainder of transcript missing}

{Transcript Missing}

DET. PRENTICE: Tell me more about the man you saw.

TINA NIX: Tall. Brown jacket. Dark pants. White hat.

DET. PRENTICE: What kind of hat?

TINA NIX: Like a baseball cap.

DET. PRENTICE: Any writing on it?

TINA NIX: None that I could make out, sorry.

DET. PRENTICE: How did he move?

TINA NIX: Sorry?

DET. PRENTICE: How did he walk? Was he fast and jerky? Slow and smooth? Did he walk like a mailman or a dog walker? A Doordash delivery person or someone looking for something?

TINA NIX: Hmm. I guess he moved kind of slowly. It might sound funny but he sort of moved like every IT guy I've ever met.

DET. PRENTICE: Can you describe that, please?

TINA NIX: Well, you know. Heavier guy. Scraggly beard.

DET. PRENTICE: Our IT guy is an Ex-Navy Seal who can squat 600 pounds.

TINA NIX: Well, you know what I mean. Let's just say this guy looked like he played a lot of video games.

DET. PRENTICE: You think the guy you saw plays video games?

TINA NIX: Maybe. Or spends a lot of time on the computer. I don't know, I think it's like, in the way they carry themselves?

DET. PRENTICE: Can you elaborate?

TINA NIX: It's all in the back. They sorta hunch but it's more than that. There's a posture in the shoulders.

DET. PRENTICE: MmmHmm.

TINA NIX: And the skin.

DET. PRENTICE: The skin.

TINA NIX: Like they don't go out in the sun a lot. Like, they might have a nice complexion if they just spent some time outside but they don't so they just look sorta...I don't know.

DET. PRENTICE: Sorta what?

TINA NIX: Sorta sallow, you know?

DET. PRENTICE: So this guy looked sallow to you?

TINA NIX: Maybe?

DET. PRENTICE: And you saw him take her?

TINA NIX: I saw him *with* her. That's about it.

DET. PRENTICE: Did you see him pull in? Did he drive?

TINA NIX: Not sure. He was just talking with Sonja when I saw him. Then I looked later and they were both gone.

DET. PRENTICE: Where were they when you saw them?

TINA NIX: On the sidewalk.

DET. PRENTICE: Which one?

TINA NIX: By the swings.

DET. PRENTICE: And where was Jennifer Bixby at this time?

TINA NIX: Sonja's mom?

DET. PRENTICE: Yes.

TINA NIX: Underneath the overhang. I think she was on her phone. Or at least, she was the few times I looked over there.

DET. PRENTICE: On her phone how?

TINA NIX: What do you mean?

DET. PRENTICE: Was she speaking with someone?

TINA NIX: No, she was texting. Or just scrolling. I don't know.

DET. PRENTICE: Did you ever get the feeling that she might know the person you saw?

TINA NIX: The man in the white hat?

DET. PRENTICE: Yes.

TINA NIX: Couldn't tell you. They never looked at each other.

DET. PRENTICE: Weren't you alarmed when you saw Sonja talking to a stranger?

TINA NIX: I don't know. I figured it was her father. I've never seen her dad before so it was my best guess. It's why I remembered it.

DET. PRENTICE: How did Sonja seem?

TINA NIX: What do you mean?

DET. PRENTICE: Was she speaking to the man the way a young girl might speak to her father or to a stranger?

TINA NIX: (laughs) I think her father might be a stranger at this point. Like I said, I've never seen the man.

DET. PRENTICE: I'd like you to try and answer the question.

TINA NIX: Sorry. Long day.

DET. PRENTICE: No worries.

TINA NIX: She seemed sort of shy. More like she was talking to a stranger, I guess. But she was just like that, you know? Whenever a grown-up was talking, she'd just stand there with her hands folded in front of her.

DET. PRENTICE: Even with her mother?

TINA NIX: Well, no, not her mother. She seemed to fight with her mother a lot.

DET. PRENTICE: How much is a lot?

TINA NIX: I don't know.

DET. PRENTICE: More than other children?

TINA NIX: Not really, I guess. They would just fight when it was time to leave. I guess those tantrums just stuck with me because of how quiet she was otherwise.

DET. PRENTICE: Okay. Is there anything else you can remember?

TINA NIX: No, not really.

DET. PRENTICE: Thank you for your time.

{Transcript Missing}

DET. PRENTICE: Would you conclude that Sonja was often the target for bullies at the park?

CHRISTINA MARTELL: Not at all. She just prefers it her way, like most children. My Trixie is no different. She might even be the main instigator in most cases.

DET. PRENTICE: Are your daughter and Sonja friends?

CHRISTINA MARTELL: Only on the playground. The girl seemed lonely. Her mother is always doing anything but paying her attention. I think she only brought her to the park to not be enclosed with her so much. Used it as a sort of getaway.

DET. PRENTICE: Do you know if any of the other families were close to the Bixbys?

CHRISTINA MARTELL: No clue, Detective. Unlikely, given the girl's shy demeanor. She seems unsure of herself. I'd assume due to the lack of a father.

DET. PRENTICE: Have you ever met the man?

CHRISTINA MARTELL: Never.

DET. PRENTICE: Ever hear Sonja mention him?

CHRISTINA MARTELL: Once. Trixie asked her where he was and she said—well, come to think of it, she said something weird.

DET. PRENTICE: How so?

CHRISTINA MARTELL: She said that her dad is always watching over her.

DET. PRENTICE: Anything else about him?

CHRISTINA MARTELL: Nothing.

DET. PRENTICE: When we began, you told me that you arrived to the park around 10:30 am, correct?

CHRISTINA MARTELL: It is.

DET. PRENTICE: Did you see the Bixbys when they arrived?

CHRISTINA MARTELL: Yes. Sonja seemed very eager to be there. She was radiating a new energy. Her mother wasn't though. She seemed as lifeless as always, if you don't mind me saying.

DET. PRENTICE: Approximate if necessary, but around what time would you say you might have noticed them?

CHRISTINA MARTELL: 11. Angelo goes on his lunch break every day at that time and gets to the park about ten after, every time. We get forty minutes, then he is back to work. He is starting his own business in the Fall. We are very excited about him being home more often.

DET. PRENTICE: How many times a week do you visit the park at Whiteset Creek?

CHRISTINA MARTELL: Two or three, pending the weather. When it permits, we like to be there. I waitress part-time, so we try to make it a routine occasion.

DET. PRENTICE: How often would you guess that the Bixbys attend?

CHRISTINA MARTELL: We see them a few times a month maybe. Hard to really say. We never really interacted too much.

DET. PRENTICE: Can you recall anything out of the ordinary this morning?

CHRISTINA MARTELL: A van was parked by the swing sets. It was there when we got there. I don't remember seeing it after the girl's mother began calling her name.

DET. PRENTICE: What time would you think she noticed her daughter missing?

CHRISTINA MARTELL: We had just finished our lunch, maybe 11:30?

DET. PRENTICE: Did you see anyone with Sonja prior to that?

CHRISTINA MARTELL: I can't say. I was enjoying the moment with my family. My husband is the more observant one.

DET. PRENTICE: That's fine, we will speak with him. If there's anything else--

CHRISTINA MARTELL: Wait... Trixie had taken the girl two cookies. Trixie may be a brat, but she sure loves to share. When I asked her why she took two, she claimed that the little girl was meeting her boyfriend for the first time.

DET. PRENTICE: Boyfriend?

CHRISTINA MARTELL: That's what she said. I brushed it off as kids pretending but then the next thing I know, the girl's mother is looking for her, then I see her on the news.

DET. PRENTICE: You said Trixie said, "Meeting him for the first time"?

CHRISTINA MARTELL: What do you think that means? You don't think this is an internet thing, do you? Like she met some guy online?

DET. PRENTICE: It's possible. An online boyfriend. The girl was only eleven... They just keep getting interested younger and younger.

CHRISTINA MARTELL: I truly pray that you locate the girl unharmed.

DET. PRENTICE: Me too. You've definitely helped. Thank you for coming in to see me.

{Transcript Missing}

DET. PRENTICE: And do you often visit Whiteset?

ANGELO MARTELL: As much as possible. My family loves two things dearly, one another and the outdoors.

DET. PRENTICE: What time would you say that you arrived this morning?

ANGELO MARTELL: 11:10 or so, almost always unless there's a detour or other traffic delay. Roads were clear this morning.

DET. PRENTICE: When you got to the park, did anything stand out to you as unordinary?

ANGELO MARTELL: There was a rugged Chrysler van parked by the swings. Have a sneaking suspicion that it was that guy, you know?

DET. PRENTICE: The one who took her?

ANGELO MARTELL: No, I saw that one.

DET. PRENTICE: You saw... hold on, back up, what guy were you first referring to?

ANGELO MARTELL: The myth about the protector, you know?

DET. PRENTICE: I don't. Enlighten me, please.

ANGELO MARTELL: Old tales spoke about a man in a hooded sweatshirt that would sit on benches near playgrounds. Nobody knew why, nor who he was. He wouldn't speak when approached. Witnesses couldn't even give matching details, but lots of people encountered him.

DET. PRENTICE: What happened to him?

ANGELO MARTELL: Nobody knows. Some say he would catch the predators and he got himself caught disposing of a body.

DET. PRENTICE: Hmm.

ANGELO MARTELL: You think I'm crazy, don't you?

DET. PRENTICE: I'm not here to make that judgment. I just need to know what you saw. Furthermore, if there are local legends floating around, I'd like to hear those too. I'll be honest and say that we don't put much stock in that sort of thing around here but these stories start somewhere. Occasionally there's a kernel of truth in them.

ANGELO MARTELL: Maybe so.

DET. PRENTICE: Have you personally seen this man?

ANGELO MARTELL: Not personally, no.

DET. PRENTICE: But, you say you saw the man who took Sonja Bixby?

ANGELO MARTELL: I believe so. I tried to tell one of your officers but he acted like he didn't even hear me. We've been sitting on our hands for the last eleven hours.

DET. PRENTICE: I'm truly sorry about that. I'll definitely have to pass that information along. Now, please continue, if you would.

ANGELO MARTELL: Trixie had just taken some cookies over and back. She was talking to Chris, but I was busy watching a man who had approached Sonja.

DET. PRENTICE: What made you start your observation?

ANGELO MARTELL: Just society. Too many children are treated like objects and not a lot seem to care. I don't know the girl well, but she's somebody to me anyway. In school they used to tease me and say things like, "softie", you know?

DET. PRENTICE: Did the girl seem leery of him?

ANGELO MARTELL: Not really. She was a little stiff upon approach, but then she went with him with ease seconds later. I thought maybe it was her dad, or maybe an uncle she hadn't seen in a while.

DET. PRENTICE: Have you ever seen Sonja's dad?

ANGELO MARTELL: Never.

DET. PRENTICE: Sonja ever say anything about him? To your daughter, maybe?

ANGELO MARTELL: Just that he's always watching over her. I sorta took that to mean he was dead, you know?

DET. PRENTICE: What can you tell me about the man you saw with Sonja?

ANGELO MARTELL: Firstly, he knew her name. We weren't too close to the swing sets but he called her by her full name, pretty sure. It was all I heard before she went with him. He looked tall, wore darker-colored clothes. A white ball cap with something on it, maybe a logo or labeling of some kind. He moved slowly, talking with the girl as she smiled and went along. If they were strangers, they fooled me. She seemed comfortable with him, he was even holding her wrist.

DET. PRENTICE: Not her hand?

ANGELO MARTELL: I assumed because she was holding the cookies...but now that I think back, they were still in the other hand.

DET. PRENTICE: Anything else?

ANGELO MARTELL: He had an unkempt beard, hunched over shoulders kind of. Seemed not to care that anyone saw her leaving with him. They both appeared comfortable to me. The girl was known for outbursts when having to leave, but not this time.

DET. PRENTICE: It's okay, Mr. Martell. Not your fault this guy did what he did.

ANGELO MARTELL: Is she dead?

DET. PRENTICE: We are still looking. I am holding out hope. We always should until there's no longer a reason to.

ANGELO MARTELL: Yeah. Just tough not to feel some guilt.

DET. PRENTICE: You've been a tremendous help in the investigation by being here. You're doing your part.

ANGELO MARTELL: Just hoping for a happy ending for once, you know?

DET. PRENTICE: Where was Jennifer during all this?

ANGELO MARTELL: Who?

DET. PRENTICE: Sonja's mom.

ANGELO MARTELL: Oh. Never paid her much mind, she seemed distant to the girl any time I ever seen them around.

DET. PRENTICE: Anything else that you think might be useful, it all counts, say it. The vague details can break a case.

ANGELO MARTELL: There is one more thing I could mention.

DET. PRENTICE: Please.

ANGELO MARTELL: The van was gone too after the mother began asking around if her daughter had been seen.

DET. PRENTICE: Is it possible that Sonja and this man entered it?

ANGELO MARTELL: Maybe but I seem to remember them walking by it, not towards it. Other than that, I can't really think of any other details.

DET. PRENTICE: Thank you for your time. You keep Trixie safe out there.

Police Communications Dispatch Transcript
4-16-3:23 am

[OFFICER] Dispatch, this is Officer Rollins, badge number 16841, reporting a possible 10-54 at the South Pier by Poplar and 7th. Please assist.

[DISPATCH] Copy that, Officer Rollins. Are there any signs of foul play or immediate danger at the scene?

[OFFICER] Negative. We've got a body but it's been long unresponsive. Witness who flagged us down says he saw a man fleeing west towards Oak Street. Medium build with a gray hoodie. I'd send a car but don't get your hopes up.

[DISPATCH] Understood. I'll dispatch someone to take a look and send emergency personnel to your location. Please secure the area and await further instructions.

[OFFICER] Roger that. And, uh--dispatch?

[DISPATCH] Yes?

[OFFICER] Give the folks you send out here a heads up. This one's ugly.

[DISPATCH] Will do, Officer Rollins. Stay safe out there.

{End of Transcript}

Interview with Harlow Gregg

Q=Det. Curtis Nolan

A=Harlow Gregg

***=Pause

Q. Today is April 16th, 2023. The time is, uh--1:15 pm. We are in interview room number one at the headquarters of the Glenview Police Department. I am Detective Curtis Nolan, badge number 16743. I am interviewing Harlow Gregg, date of birth 7-6-1981. Harlow, are you aware that this interview is being recorded?

A. I am.

Q. And do you acknowledge that you were previously advised of your constitutional rights, that you signed a statement that detailed those rights, and that you agreed to speak to us without an attorney present?

A. I do.

Q. Alright, tell me about this morning.

A. Well, I was getting my cart ready when I noticed some guy down by the pier. He had a big bag and looked like he was about to throw it over the edge down into the water. I called out to him.

Q. Your cart. You mean your hotdog cart?

A. Correct.

Q. Do you often get your cart ready at 3 in the morning?

A. I do, as a matter of fact. Tons of fisherman coming down there between 4 and 5. And lots of times, the granola bar they had earlier ain't cuttin' it. Know what I'm saying?

Q. Okay, and you said you saw someone while you were setting up?

A. I did.

Q. And you called out to them?

A. That's what I said.

Q. What made you do that?

A. Like I said, he looked suspicious with that big bag and everything. I've seen enough television shows to know what a body dump looks like.

Q. Most people would think that the bag we recovered at the scene wasn't big enough for a body.

A. Not an adult one, no.

Q. Can you elaborate?

A. Man, I watch the news. I know y'all are running around crazy looking for that girl.

Q. And you thought it might be her in there?

A. I don't know what I thought. I just saw something fishy going down and wanted to stop it.

Q. Weren't you afraid for your safety?

A. I was, yeah.

***

Q. You look like you want to say something.

A. Okay, yeah. I wasn't going to call out to him at first. I was just watching.

Q. No? What made you do it?

A. Well, as he was walking up to drop the bag, he turns and sees me. Now, I can't see his eyes under there but I know we made eye contact. You feel?

Q. I do. Go on.

A. As soon as we lock gazes, I start yelling at him. Shouting "hey" and asking what he's got. What he's doing. To be honest, I was just making noise. I was hoping someone else would hear me, look out their window, and see what was going on.

Q. Did they?

A. You know the answer to that.

Q. I'd like to hear it from you.

A. Yeah, Big Tucker heard. He lives above the bait shop on 7th Street and sure enough, a couple seconds after I start yellin' he flips all the lights on upstairs and leans out the window.

Q. What happened then?

A. The guy looks at me. Then he looks at Tucker, who is running down onto the main level now and throwing on the shop lights. So he--ffffft--skedaddles.

Q. He runs.

A. Yeah.

Q. And the bag?

A. He drops it.

Q. Where? When?

A. Right where he's standing and as soon as he can.

Q. He doesn't walk over and drop it in the water?

A. He thought about it.

Q. What makes you say that?

A. He looked over towards the rail. Then looked back. Then he
    dropped it and took off.

Q. Why do you think he left it?

A. Maybe it was too far. He was maybe...twenty feet from the
    water's edge?

Q. Maybe.

A. Yeah.

Q. But you don't think so.

A. Why do you say that?

Q. You don't think so.

A. Okay, you're right. I don't think so.

Q. What do you think?

A. I think the water suddenly wasn't a good idea.

Q. You think he changed his mind?

A. What do you mean?

Q. He was going to dispose of the body. Then he wasn't.

A. I think he did the math.

Q. What do you mean?

A. I think he saw me. Heard Big Tucker coming out. He knew
    we'd either fish the bag out of the water or point the cops at
    it anyway. So he cut his losses and ran.

Q. And?

A. Man, why you think there's an "and?"

Q. I don't think anything. But you do.

A. Fine. I think he wanted someone to find it.

Q. Why would he want that?

A. I think he wanted people to open up that bag. I think he wanted someone to see what he did. I think he was sending a message.

Q. And what message do you think that might be?

A. I've heard the rumors.

Q. Rumors?

A. You know what I'm talking about.

Q. Can you go ahead and state it for the record?

A. No, I don't think I will. I don't wanna be hauled in five months from now as a witness for some IA case about leaked information.

Q. That's not how this works.

A. I don't care how this works. But I'll tell you this: I think he dropped that bag as a warning. I think he wanted the next guy who thinks about taking a kid off the street to reconsider.

Q. To reconsider?

A. Yeah. I think he wanted the next guy to imagine himself being found like that.

Q. Like what?

A. Like he was mauled by a pack of wolves. I think he wanted the next guy to imagine himself being found in a duffle bag like a butchered hog.

{Remainder of transcript missing}

{Transcript Missing}

A. He looked normal. I don't know what else to tell you.

Q. What was his face like? Thick? Narrow? Did he have a big nose or a small one? What color were his eyes? Details, Mr. Wessel. All you can give.

A. Too dark to tell eye color. Everything else was just average. Nose was neither big nor small. Face wasn't too thick or thin. He looked like a template for a person.

Q. Any ethnicity you could discern?

A. No, he kind of looked white when I first saw him but the more I looked the less sure I was.

Q. But you think he was white?

A. That's not what I said.

Q. You gotta give me something here.

A. Like I said, I don't know what to tell you. Type "human man" into any image search engine and this guy's face comes up.

Q. So you see him come around the corner. You make eye contact. What then?

A. Nothing.

Q. Nothing.

A. Yeah. Dude just gives me the nod and keeps walking.

Q. He look out of breath to you?

A. Not really.

Q. Okay, thanks for coming in. We appreciate your--

A. You know who he was?

Q. Do I know who he was? No, I don't suppose I do. That's why you're sitting on the other side of this table.

A. Not what he looked like. Who he was?

Q. I'm not sure I know what you're getting at.

A. I bet my bottom dollar it was the girl.

Q. What girl?

A. You know, *the* girl. The Bixby girl.

Q. Sonja Bixby?

A. Yeah, man.

Q. Are you telling me you think an eleven year old girl dressed up as an adult man and that's who you ran into on the street?

A. Not dressed up. She's a shapeshifter, dude. One of them skinchangers.

***

A. You're looking at me like you think I'm crazy.

Q. I think you spend too much of your time on internet forums.

A. How do you explain it then? Fairway has a camera right out in front of their shop a block down from where I saw your guy. There's no footage of him passing by. But, there is footage of an elderly woman in similar clothes passing by about when he could have been there. Or no, correction: should have been there.

Q. Similar clothes, yes. But not the same. Her shoes were an off-white and other witness accounts have the guy wearing dark brown hiking boots.

A. Pfft. Eyewitness accounts. You know how reliable those are.

Q. Boy, do I.

A. Hey brother, I take offense to that. And I've seen the footage. We ain't exactly watching the Sunday replays here. Those could just as easily have been hiking boots with a sheen on them from the overhead lights. And what do you think about the hoodie?

Q. What about the hoodie?

A. It was the same one.

Q. There are about a billion grey hoodies in this town. Walk outside and you can probably point at seven of them.

A. You don't look so certain.

Q. What about the timeline?

A. What about it?

Q. If Sonja Bixby had the power to free herself, then why not do it sooner? Why wait three days?

A. Maybe she didn't know she could do it. Maybe she was pushed to it.

Q. Okay...

A. Or maybe it wasn't her that was being held! Maybe it started that way but she turned the tables. Maybe she held her abductor for three days.

Q. Doing what?

A. Doing whatever she did to him that made it so she could shove him inside of a standard-size duffle bag.

***

A. What?

Q. Hey Prentice, they do the press conference yet?

{Sound of door opening}

P. They should just be finishing up.

Q. Okay, thanks.

{Sound of door closing}

A. What was that about?

Q. I wasn't sure about telling you this but they just covered it in the press conference, so what the hell?

A. I'm listening.

Q. They think the video from the boutique that's floating around is AI-generated.

A. They think?

Q. It is.

A. You said, "They think."

Q. 87% certainty is what the software says. Now go on your little forums and share that, please. You can quote me.

A. I'm not buying it.

Q. I don't expect you to. But it doesn't matter. What matters is that the footage was leaked online by an unknown profile. The shop owners have a camera but they deny uploading anything.

A. You get the footage from that camera to look at yourself?

Q. We did.

A. And?

Q. And nothing.

A. If it was nothing, you'd tell me that you looked and matched the timestamps and that there was nothing. You'd have said that right away.

Q. Okay, I think we're done here.

A. The footage for that time is missing, isn't it? Or it's corrupted somehow.

Q. Do you have anything else for me?

A. Nope. Just saying, you guys gotta watch out. You got a killer out there that can look like anyone at any time.

Q. Thank you for your time, Mr. Wessel. We'll be in touch.

{Transcript Missing}

DET. PRENTICE: What were you doing out that way so early in the morning?

JANEL MELROSE: The same alibi I have every night at that time, I was moon-gambling off of South Pier.

DET. PRENTICE: One of those, huh? Describe what happened. Every detail is of importance.

JANEL MELROSE: I was with my best friend, Eliana Meade, who has like the weakest bladder.

DET. PRENTICE: Were you two drinking?

JANEL MELROSE: No. We are more about peyote buttons, but were totally sober last night.

DET. PRENTICE: That's very, uh...forthcoming of you.

JANEL MELROSE: You said *every* detail.

DET. PRENTICE: Go on.

JANEL MELROSE: So, she did her business, then she comes back and tells me that she saw a guy wearing a hoodie briskly walking towards the Pier with a heavy duffle bag. At this point, I'm thinking bags of cash, you know? Maybe jewelry from a heist gone bad that they were trying to ditch.

DET. PRENTICE: Jewelry that you were going to report to us, right?

JANEL MELROSE: Of course.

DET. PRENTICE: Yeah. Go on.

JANEL MELROSE: So we like, freak out and try to follow him. He gets near the Pier and is looking to toss it over when the hotdog guy yells at him. He stopped and stood there clutching the bag. Then Big Tucker came out of his house so we hid and watched. He had a ball bat in his hand. The man took off sprinting and left the bag behind.

{Transcript Missing}

Interviewer: Det. Curtis Nolan

4-16-2023/3:45 pm

Case # 36-117

Interview with Jennifer Bixby

Q=Det. Curtis Nolan

A=Jennifer Bixby

L=Cole Wexlend (Lawyer)

***=Pause

Q. Today is April 16th, 2023. The time is 3:45 pm. We are in interview room number one at the headquarters of the Glenview Police Department. I am Detective Curtis Nolan, badge number 16743. I am interviewing Jennifer Bixby, date of birth 9-22-1994. Ms. Bixby, are you aware that this interview is being recorded?

A. Yes.

Q. Do you acknowledge that you were previously advised of your constitutional rights, that you signed a statement that detailed those rights, and that you are here with your attorney present?

A. Yes.

Q. What is your relation to the missing person, Sonja Bixby?

A. Her mother.

Q. Biological?

A. Yes.

Q. And her father?

A. I'd rather not talk about him.

Q. Do you have reason to believe that he may be involved in her abduction?

A. The abduction? No.

Q. Do you have more to add?

A. I'd rather not.

Q. Do you fear your ex, Ms. Bixby?

A. No. For neither me nor Sonja. He was a good man, but he has his ways.

Q. Can you elaborate on what that means?

L. My client respectfully stated she does not want to discuss the man.

A. Sometimes, I swear that I saw those ways in Sonja.

Q. In what ways, Ms. Bixby?

L. Detective Nolan, you're treading dangerous ground...

A. I'm unsure that Sonja going missing isn't what's best if his ways were coming through.

Q. Did you have something to do with her disappearance?

L: Detective!

***

Q. Do you agree that we can discuss the day your daughter went missing?

A. Yes.

Q. Can you tell me what time you arrived at the park? An approximation is fine.

A. 11 a.m., sharp. Sonja was insistent on us being punctual that day. We covered this in the initial interview.

Q. Is that unusual behavior for her?

A. A little bit, yes. She doesn't usually pay so much attention to time frames like she did that day.

Q. Did she have access to the internet? A social media account?

A. Yes.

Q. To?

A. All of it. It's not unheard of to see kids on their tablets instead of on the playground equipment.

Q. Did you ever monitor her activity?

A. Not enough hours in the day, Detective.

Q. Did she keep in touch with Mr. Bixby on the devices?

L. Nolan...

A. I'm unaware what she doing when she in front of her screens, okay. I already told you.

Q. Some frequent parkgoers mentioned that there were conflicts with Sonja and some of the other kids.

A. Sometimes.

Q. Can you tell me more about that?

A. Just the nonsense of children. Disputes over minor things.

Q. Would you consider you and Sonja to be close, Ms. Bixby?

A. No. I mean I'd like to be but she just reminds me so much of him.

L. Jennifer...

A. Seriously though. I'd never do anything to hurt her. But she scares me sometimes.

Q. Scared you how?

A. She just did.

Q. Any examples?

A. No.

Q. Okay. So, when you say "him" you mean Sonja's father?

A. Yes.

L. Careful, Detective...

Q. Would you consider either of them dangerous?

A. I do not wish to answer.

Q. Did you and Mr. Bixby separate due to violence in the home?

A. Not in the home, no.

Q. Violent towards others outside of the family then?

A. I decline to answer.

Q. Do you think your ex could be capable of harming his daughter?

A. No.

Q. Would he have any reason to want her out of the way?

A. No.

Q. How about you? Several statements were made that you were often seen in public arguing with her.

L. Detective, I think we have had enough of this. My client and I are leaving. Interrogating a grieving mother, you should be ashamed, Nolan.

Q: You said "was" in reference to your ex earlier? Why, Ms. Bixby?

A: You'd never comprehend his transcendence, just as I never could.

Q: What does that mean, is he alive or dead?!

L: Let's go, enough of this charade!

ends transcript

Interview with Saul Dod

Q = Det. Curtis Nolan

A = Saul Dod

*** = Pause

Q. Today is April 16th, 2023 and the time is 7:55 pm. We are in interview room number three at the headquarters of the Glenview Police Department. I am Detective Curtis Nolan, badge number 16743. I am interviewing Saul Dod, date of birth, 2-28-2002. Mr. Dod, are you aware that this interview is being recorded?

A. Yeah.

Q. And do you acknowledge that you were previously advised of your constitutional rights, that you signed a statement that detailed those rights, and that you agreed to speak to us without an attorney present?

A. Do I need one? I'm innocent, swear it.

Q. Relax. This is just a formal questioning because you came forward as having seen a missing person.

A. Yeah. It was that girl who has been all over the TV. She was with some old dude yesterday at the gas station at the intersection of Highway 72 and Poplar Boulevard.

Q. Did she seem fearful of the man that she was with?

A. Not at all. She was anxiously asking about somebody named... Brian, or Bradley... no, Brandon.

Q. No last name?

A. Not that I heard, but I wasn't eavesdropping either. I didn't realize who she was at first, but after they left, I saw her photo on the front page of the paper and it clicked.

Q. Nothing at all seemed to throw a red flag about their interactions? Think for a minute, Saul.

A. Yeah. Actually, I did see that he had a firm grasp on her wrist. Her left, I want to say.

Q. So then he was primarily using his left hand?

A. Yeah, dude was a leftie.

Q. Do you think you could identify him if you saw him in a lineup?

A. Probably. Y'all catch him?

Q. We will.

A. No saying what a creep like that is doing to her, better hurry up. They don't always look like you'd think. I thought they were related. He was smoothly walking with her like she was his.

Q. That's a disturbing thought.

A. Yeah, but it's a fact, dude.

Q. Did you happen to see what type of vehicle they got in?

A. Nah. Don't the place have cameras?

Q. Six months out of order, according to the owner.

A. Dude, that sucks.

Q. It doesn't help. So, other than mentioning a Brandon, did the girl or the man say anything else?

A. He told her that Brandon was really starting to like her, maybe too much, and that it was becoming a problem.

Q. Nauseating. Did you take it to mean that he was this Brandon?

A. Yeah. Dude is sick. I mean, obviously.

Q. Did the girl have any injuries that you could see? Any marks anywhere?

A. Nah, not that I saw. She just seemed very ready to meet Brandon, but like I stated, I thought the old dude *was* Brandon. I think better after a smoke, take five?

***

Q. Feel better?

A. Always do after my lungs are open, dude. Thanks for the break.

Q. Sure. Did they buy anything while in the gas station?

A. Buy? Nah. I did see the old dude pocket a package of zip ties though. No purchase needed. He just straight five-finger discounted 'em.

Q. Anything else?

A. Hmm... oh, after it hit me who she was, I read the article and I'm fairly that certain she was in the exact same outfit they described. So, I'd guess that old dude hadn't taken her where he needed to yet. At the very least, I don't think she had been unclothed.

Q. Makes sense with the stolen zip ties. Very insightful, Mr. Dod, I truly appreciate you coming forward with this information.

A. Dude, even the hardest defend kids. I just wish I had stopped him somehow. Best of luck, dude, you know how this typically ends.

Police Communications Dispatch Transcript
4-17-2023, 2:25 am

[DISPATCH] Dispatch to all units, we have a caller reporting an abandoned but idling vehicle out on Highway 72, east of South Pier.

[OFFICER] Dispatch, this is Eads, I'm heading to that location. I'm a few miles west of there. Standby.

[OFFICER] Dispatch, this is Officer Eads, badge number 16950, I am on the scene out here on Highway 72 with an abandoned brown Chrysler in rough shape. No plates. I am just east of South Pier. I have eyes on the caller and situation. I am approaching now. Please, stand by.

[DISPATCH] Copy, Officer Eads. Keep me advised as to what is happening.

[OFFICER] Dispatch, there is a little girl inside of this van. I shut off the engine and am going to approach the child inside.

[DISPATCH] Copy, what's her condition? Do you need Medical?

[OFFICER] Negative. She says she was unharmed. I think it might be that girl.

[DISPATCH] Which girl, officer?

[OFFICER] The Bixby girl.

[DISPATCH] Copy, ask her what her name is.

[OFFICER] Yep. She says her name is Sonja Bixby.

[DISPATCH] Oh my god.

[OFFICER] Yeah, I know.

[DISPATCH] Can you ask where she was?

[OFFICER] She says that she was supposed to meet her boyfriend Brandon, but instead his grandpa took her to a basement to wait for him.

[DISPATCH] Are we sure she is okay?

[OFFICER] She'll need to be checked out by emergency but from the looks of it, yeah. She is in the same clothes that she was last seen wearing. No marks or signs of trauma. She's saying that she got confused when the grandpa started claiming he was Brandon and knew facts that only they had discussed. She promises the abductor never did anything inappropriate to her, but it did frighten her when nobody her age was around at the house she was taken to.

[DISPATCH] Copy. Did she say how she managed to escape?

{Transcript Missing}

To those in waiting,

Sonja Bixby was found the morning of April 17th, 2023. She had no physical wounds of any kind, yet she refused to speak about what had happened. When asked directly, she said that she went off to meet her online boyfriend but that things didn't work out and they quickly split up. Even under an intense barrage of questioning, she refused to elaborate further.

Soon after, the body of Dexter Lingon was ID'd by family after being dumped in a duffle bag two days before by the South Pier. His limbs and head were all roughly severed and stacked in the bag. Soft tissues had deep lacerations and showed signs of biting and heavy sucking.

Upon inspection of Lingon's residence, hair and fibers from three previous missing persons were found along with pieces of jewelry and clothing from another eleven. More items are still being cross-referenced with other missing persons cases. As of today, none of the victims or their bodies have been found.

Members of our organization did their own follow-up interviews with some of the witnesses in the Sonja Bixby case nearly a year later, and while hardly anything of further substance was produced, there is one interview that stood out. It was taken in the corner booth of an undisclosed bar and the interviewee did not know he was being recorded.

While this breach of trust was regrettable, the truth must shine on if it is to illuminate the path ahead. Due to background noise, however, only parts of the conversation are intelligible. What follows is the transcript from that conversation.

Blessings,
SwordMouth

Q: Interviewer

A: Detective Curtis Nolan

Q: Good evening.

A: Look, I need you to stop going around running your mouth about the Sonja Bixby case. You have no idea what you're talking about.

Q: I'm just trying to find the truth, Detective. Would you like a drink?

A: No. And don't wave at the bartender. The less people who know I'm here the better.

Q: You seem afraid.

A: Damn right, I'm afraid. You don't know the kind of people you're getting involved with.

Q: They've all seemed pretty nice so far. Can't remember much and everyone has their own theories, but—

A: No, not the witnesses. I mean whoever it is you stole this information from in the first place. And don't deny it. They came in here with shredders and garbage bags and cleaned out our evidence lockers and file cabinets. Said they were with the NSA but I don't think so. These guys didn't walk and talk like a bunch of pencil-pushers. They moved like us. Like *cops*. Except they all had shark eyes.

Q: What do you mean by "shark eyes?"

A: I mean like, if one of 'em got a text on their phone that told them to line us all up against the wall and put bullets in our heads, they'd do it without blinking and then go grab some Cokes and subs from the nearby deli afterward.

Q; What do you think they have to do with the case?

A: Not sure. They—

{indephirable}

Q:—by the docks?

A: Yeah, whoever it was, they found him and put the screws to him. Pliers, jumper cables, the whole gambit. Must have thought he knew something because they took him *apart*.

Q: And you think they'd do the same to you? Even though you're a cop?

A: They don't care. I'll tell you one thing though, they're not the only players out there. And I'm not talking about you folks.

Q: What do you mean?

A: I mean, one of the guys I saw in here emptying out file cabinets and digging through all our desks and stuff? Well, get this: his body showed up down by the train tracks three weeks later. Made Wessel's body look downright tidy. Only reason we knew who it was was because Prentice said he recognized the watch and the two moles on the guy's inner wrist.

Q: He was able to identify him with that little?

A; Prentice is an accessories hound. Probably clocked the moles while he was checking out the watch. Good luck for us too, because the guy is still sitting in the morgue as a John Doe. He's a ghost. No trace of him in the system.

Q: Couldn't you call the guys who flipped your office? Tell them you got their boy?

A: How? They didn't exactly leave their business cards.

Q: They didn't show you ID?

A: They showed *someone* ID but it sure wasn't me. Either way, we got no idea who to go to with this. Seems like no one wants to touch it.

Q: What do you think happened?

A: I think those guys read our interviews. Saw something in our conversation with Wessel that they recognized and we didn't. They caught up with him, tortured the info out, and then dumped his carcass in a cornfield.

Q: Then what?

A: Then they actually found the guy.

Q: The guy?

A: Or gal. Or monster. Who knows? Either way, I think one of their boys grabbed the snake by the tip of the tail and caught the fangs, if you know what I mean.

Q: You think whoever butchered Sonja's kidnapper killed one of your NSA impersonators?

A: Butcher isn't the word for it. This guy was turned inside out. We found his guts hanging in a pine tree twenty-five feet away like tinsel at Christmas time. Make no mistake: whoever or *whatever* did this is a monster. This wasn't self-defense we're talking about here. This was bloodlust. There was a kind of frenetic energy I've only read about in serial killer case files. The worst of the worst, I'm telling you. This was utter brutality on a scale you've never seen before. And ya know what?

Q: What?

A: Whatever this thing is, it looks like you and me. And it's still out there.

{indephirable}

Also by Christopher Besonen

NETWORK: A Technological, Imaginative Horror Novella

Find out Besonen's thoughts on the Indie Horror books he is reading at Uncomfortably Dark

Also by Fredrick Niles

Crimes of the Blood Cults: An Occult Noir Short Story Collection

Follow Fredrick Niles on his Substack, Outpost for Gargoyles, where he talks about Myth, Monsters, and Meaning-Making

About the authors

Christopher Besonen can usually be found in either Missouri or Ohio depending on the year. He is the author of 10 books that create a Puzzle Series. The more you read, the more pieces connect. All titles can also work as standalone.

Linktr.ee/BesonenHorror

Besonen is on most social platforms: #BesonenHorror

***

Fredrick Niles is the author of *Ash Above, Snow Below* and *The Omen Tree*. He lives in St. Paul, Minnesota where he writes fiction and plays music. In his free time he rants about movies, lurks in bookstores, and practices introversion with his wife.